Disney
PRINCESS
Palace
pets

Belle's Playful Puppy

by Amy Sky Koster

illustrated by the Disney Storybook Art Team

Random House 🏠 New York

Meet Teacup!
She is a puppy.

She puts on a show.

People clap.

The people give
Teacup treats!

Princess Belle sees Teacup.

The sun is bright.

It gets in Teacup's eyes.

Teacup drops her cup.

She is sad.

Belle helps Teacup.

Teacup hugs Belle.

She likes the princess!

Belle takes Teacup home.

Teacup is her new pet!

Soon, Teacup is ready
to do her show again.

She runs toward
the town.
She goes through
the woods.

She makes new friends
in the woods.

Teacup puts on a show
for her new friends!

Teacup is ready to go to the town.

She gets lost!

Teacup hears a noise.

She is scared.

It is Petit!

She is looking for Teacup.

Petit gives Teacup glasses.
They will block the sun!

Petit takes Teacup

to the town square.

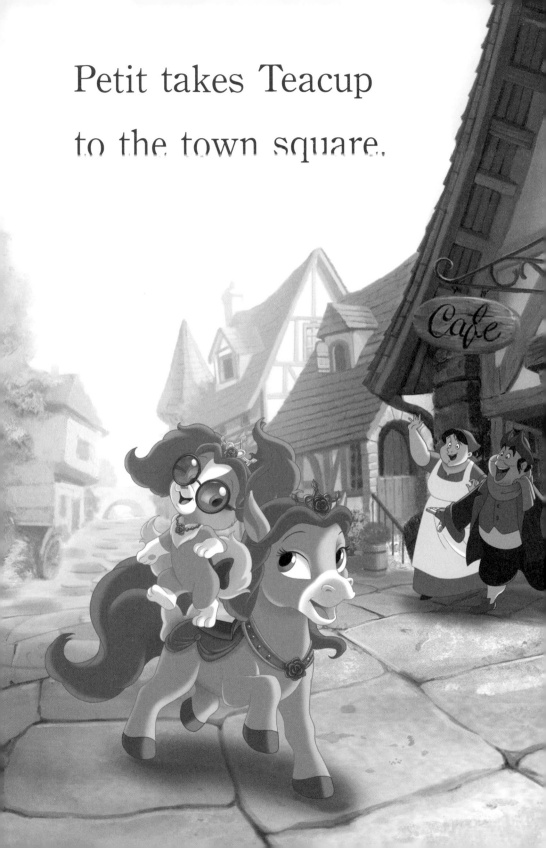

Teacup and Petit put on
a great show together!

Teacup has many
new friends.
Hooray!

Dear Parents:

Congratulations! Your child is taking the first steps on an exciting journey. The destination? Independent reading!

STEP INTO READING® will help your child get there. The program offers five steps to reading success. Each step includes fun stories and colorful art or photographs. In addition to original fiction and books with favorite characters, there are Step into Reading Non-Fiction Readers, Phonics Readers and Boxed Sets, Sticker Readers, and Comic Readers—a complete literacy program with something to interest every child.

Learning to Read, Step by Step!

Ready to Read   Preschool–Kindergarten
• big type and easy words • rhyme and rhythm • picture clues
For children who know the alphabet and are eager to begin reading.

Reading with Help   Preschool–Grade 1
• basic vocabulary • short sentences • simple stories
For children who recognize familiar words and sound out new words with help.

Reading on Your Own   Grades 1–3
• engaging characters • easy-to-follow plots • popular topics
For children who are ready to read on their own.

Reading Paragraphs   Grades 2–3
• challenging vocabulary • short paragraphs • exciting stories
For newly independent readers who read simple sentences with confidence.

Ready for Chapters   Grades 2–4
• chapters • longer paragraphs • full-color art
For children who want to take the plunge into chapter books but still like colorful pictures.

STEP INTO READING® is designed to give every child a successful reading experience. The grade levels are only guides; children will progress through the steps at their own speed, developing confidence in their reading.

Remember, a lifetime love of reading starts with a single step!

Step into Reading, Random House, and the Random House colophon are registered trademarks
of Penguin Random House LLC.

Visit us on the Web!
StepIntoReading.com
rhcbooks.com

Educators and librarians, for a variety of teaching tools, visit us at RHTeachersLibrarians.com

ISBN 978-0-7364-4258-9 (trade) — ISBN 978-0-7364-9010-8 (lib. bdg.)
ISBN 978-0-7364-4259-6 (ebook)

Printed in the United States of America

10 9 8 7 6 5 4 3 2 1

Random House Children's Books supports the First Amendment and celebrates the right to read.